D0297611

margaret Tempest.

THE KNOT
SQUIRREL TIED

BY ALISON UTTLEY

PICTURES BY
MARGARET TEMPEST

Collins

First published in Great Britain by
William Collins Sons & Co in 1937
This edition published by
HarperCollins Publishers Ltd in 1993
Text copyright © The Alison Uttley
Literary Property Trust 1988
Illustrations copyright
© The Estate of Margaret Tempest 1988
Copyright this arrangement
© William Collins Sons & Co Ltd 1988

Illustration on p.4 by Mary Cooper
Alison Uttley's original story
has been abridged for this book.

A CIP catalogue record for this title
is available from the British Library.

ISBN: 0 00 194263 8

All rights reserved. No part of this
publication may be reproduced,
stored in a retrieval system, or
transmitted in any form or by any
means, electronic, mechanical,
photocopying, recording or otherwise,
without the prior permission of
HarperCollins Publishers Ltd,
77-85 Fulham Palace Road,
Hammersmith, London W6 8JB

Printed and bound in Italy

This book is set in Goudy

Collins

An Imprint of HarperCollins*Publishers*

FOREWORD

Of course you must understand that Grey Rabbit's home had no electric light or gas, and even the candles were made from pith of rushes dipped in wax from the wild bees' nests, which Squirrel found. Water there was in plenty, but it did not come from a tap. It flowed from a spring outside, which rose up from the ground and went to a brook. Grey Rabbit cooked on a fire, but it was a wood fire, there was no coal in that part of the country. Tea did not come from India, but from a little herb known very well to country people, who once dried it and used it in their cottage homes. Bread was baked from wheat ears, ground fine, and Hare and Grey Rabbit gleaned in the cornfields to get the wheat.

The doormats were plaited rushes, like country-made mats, and cushions were stuffed with wool gathered from the hedges where sheep pushed through the thorns. As for the looking-glass, Grey Rabbit found the glass, dropped from a lady's handbag, and Mole made a frame for it. Usually the animals gazed at themselves in the still pools as so many country children have done. The country ways of Grey Rabbit were the country ways known to the author.

One morning Rat came to his house door and gazed up and down with a weary eye. Then he slowly hobbled out to the hazel spinney and made a crutch to help himself along.

Mrs Rat shut the door after him, and sighed as she rocked the wicker cradle in which her baby lay.

"Hush-a-bye," she sang in a high shrill voice.

"Father Rat will bring thee an egg,
He'll either steal or borrow or beg."

"Alas!" she sighed. "It has never been the same since he stole the food from Grey Rabbit's house, and that impudent Squirrel tied a knot in his tail. No one can untie it! Poor Rat! He has indeed suffered for his misdoings!"

Rat crept along under the shadow of the wall. No longer could he scamper in a light-hearted way with his tail rippling behind him. Now it dragged in the heavy knot which Squirrel had tied to remind him of his wickedness. The knot was always in the way. It got entangled in briars. It caught under doors. It thumped flip-flop! when he walked down the stairs of the farm buildings, so that dogs and cats sprang up and rushed after him. No longer could he poach or thieve or hunt.

"Every day I get thinner and thinner, I never can get a really good dinner," Rat told his friends at the Cock and Bull Inn, but they only laughed as they crept under the wainscot, and left him to thump uncomfortably after them.

At last he reached the farm buildings, and he climbed up the narrow stair into the hen-house. He knew the Speckledy Hen had laid an egg, for he had heard her cackling triumphantly, boasting to all the world, of her cleverness.

Rat crept through the little door. In one nest lay the big brown egg, which had the golden yolk Rat loved. He snatched it up, but when he started downstairs the knot in his tail caught in the doorway, and he over-balanced. At that moment the Speckledy Hen looked up from the farmyard below.

"My egg! Oh! My dear egg!" she shrieked.

Rat struggled to get free, and dropped the egg. It rolled down the stairway and spilt on the ground, and Rat rushed to safety.

"So near, and yet so far," he groaned, as he rested in a hole in the wall.

He waited till the noise had died down, then he crept into the barn where fine bags of meal stood in a corner. Here was a lucky find! He gnawed a hole in one, and had just started to eat the sweet delicious grain, when in his excitement he moved clumsily, and the knot in his tail thumped on the boards.

Bang! Like a drum it sounded, and into the barn came the farmyard cat.

What a race Rat had for the door! He only just got safely away, with his coat torn, and his felt hat left behind in the cat's claws!

"That was a near squeak," he moaned. Rat pulled his belt tighter, and sat down to think.

"Hedgehog is a kindly soul," said he to himself. "He'll give me a drink, I'm sure, and I can ask his advice."

That afternoon the Rat watched Hedgehog milk a cow. He licked his lips hungrily then stepped softly up to him.

"Mr Hedgehog," said Rat, humbly. "I never get anything to eat nowadays. My tail warns people of my coming."

"Yes," said Hedgehog. "We have all been more comfortable lately."

"I'm nearly a skellington," Rat went on, wiping his eyes with a ragged handkerchief.

The kindly Hedgehog held out a pail of milk and Rat drank it all up with eager gulps. Before Hedgehog could stop him, he had finished the second pailful too.

Hedgehog looked cross. "Now I shall have to go back to the cow," he grumbled, "and she'll stamp her foot, and moo at me."

"Please kind Hedgehog," whined Rat, "how can I get the knot undone?"

"Let me see what I can do," said the Hedgehog. "My fingers are all thumbs, but I'll use my prickles." He tugged at the knot with his spikes and Rat squealed, "Oh! Oh! Oh-oo-ooh!"

"I can't undo it, Rat," said Hedgehog. "Clever fingers fastened it. Go and ask Mole's advice. Tell him I sent you."

Mole was digging up pig-nuts in his garden.

"Good afternoon, Rat," said he. "May I ask what brings you here? You are quite a stranger, luckily."

"Please, Mole, can you untie the knot in my tail?" asked the Rat in a tiny, sad little voice. "Hedgehog couldn't loosen it, and he thought your strong hands, your digging-fingers could unfasten it."

Without a word, Mole trotted indoors and returned with a bowl of soup and a slice of bread.

"Eat this first," said he.

Rat thanked him and gobbled up the food. Then Mole seized the knot with his long pink fingers and struggled and tugged but still the knot wouldn't come undone.

"You have tightened it with dragging it after you, Rat. The only one who can help you is Wise Owl."

"I daren't go to him," said Rat shortly. "I'm scared of him. A thin rat would be nothing to a hungry owl."

"Take him a present, Rat," replied Mole. "He collects presents. Don't forget to wave your handkerchief for a truce," he added.

"I haven't got a present," said Rat, as he turned away. "I am so poor I have nothing." He put his hand in his pocket and brought out the ragged handkerchief and a bone. He looked at the bone then laughed softly.

"I haven't even a knife, but my teeth are sharp, as sharp as a razor."

He sat down on a log and gnawed at the bone. He bit a piece off here and a slip off there, and a snippet from one end, and a whiff from the other, working away, polishing and rubbing as he went. He was so much interested in his work, that night came before he had finished.

"Have you brought any food, Rat?" asked his wife, when she opened the door.

"Nothing, wife," said Rat, "but tomorrow I'm going to see Wise Owl."

He showed his wife his carving.

It was a little white ship with rigging and sails, and tiny portholes. There was a figure-head at the prow, a seagull with outstretched wings.

"I never knew you were so clever, Rat," said the admiring Mrs Rat.

The next afternoon Rat set off with his finished ship in his pocket, and a clean handkerchief.

On his way to Wise Owl's wood he had to pass little Grey Rabbit's cottage. Delicious smells came from the window, and Rat crept up to see what was being cooked. He didn't want to get to Owl's house till dusk, so there was plenty of time, and perhaps he might pick up a morsel of food, if he was careful.

Little Grey Rabbit and Squirrel were making raspberry jam tartlets.

"Grey Rabbit, Grey Rabbit," called Hare, running up the garden path and bursting into the kitchen. Rat hid under the juniper bush and Hare passed him without noticing.

"Haymaking has begun," he said. "Daisy Field is cut. Can we all go and play in the hayfield? The grass will be hay by tomorrow with this sunshine."

"Oh, let's," cried Grey Rabbit, and she waved her rolling-pin excitedly. "We'll go when the men have gone home tomorrow evening."

"I know a corner where we can make hay all by ourselves," said Squirrel, absent-mindedly putting the jam into her own mouth instead of into the patty-pans.

"We'll invite Mole and Hedgehog and Fuzzypeg," said little Grey Rabbit, "and have tea in the hayfield."

"I'll make some treacle toffee to take with us," said Hare. He took a saucepan and measured out butter and treacle and sugar. He stirred it over the fire, getting in Squirrel's way, and knocking over the flour bin. Then he ran to the garden for a pinch of lavender and sweetbrier and lad's-love, to give it a flavour. Rat held his breath. It was lucky he was as thin as a shadow, or Hare would have seen him.

"That isn't treacle toffee!" exclaimed Squirrel indignantly.

"No I've changed its name," said Hare, grinning. "It's Lavender Toffee." He stirred in his herbs, and the sweet smell came into the room, almost as strong as the raspberry jam.

Little Grey Rabbit put her tartlets in the oven, and Hare set his toffee on the window-sill to cool.

Then they all went out in the garden and sat among the flowers, sipping lemonade, and fanning themselves with the leaves of the sycamore-tree.

Rat crept up to the back door, and looked into the cosy kitchen. He knew his way about quite well.

"Ah!" he sighed, and he dragged his unwilling tail over the doorway. "I'm safe for a few minutes," said he.

He crouched down by the fire, and sniffed the savoury smells of raspberry tartlets which came from the oven. He opened the oven door and poked his nose in the hot jam.

"Oh!" he squeaked in a muffled voice. "Too hot!"

He dipped the tip of his tail in the cooling toffee, but that was too hot, also. He squirmed round and looked at the burn. The knot seemed tighter than ever.

Through the open window he heard the three friends make plans for the picnic.

"There's my chance," said Rat. "I'll come along tomorrow and see what I can find."

Then he shuffled out of the house, and went through the wood to Wise Owl's house in the great beech-tree. He rang the little silver bell which hung from the door, and the sleepy bird came to see who wanted him in the daylight.

Rat waved his handkerchief, and the Owl made a truce. "Rat!" said he gruffly. "What do you want?"

"I've brought you a present, Wise Owl." Rat spoke in a trembling voice.

Rat fumbled in his pocket and brought out the little ship.

"Hm-m," said Wise Owl, flying down and examining it. "A nice bit of carving. Pity you don't do more work, Rat. Why not try to work instead of to thieve?"

"Please, Wise Owl, will you unknot my tail?" asked Rat, humbly. "I am as thin as a leaf, and no one is clever enough to unknot me."

Owl hummed to himself.

"I'm afraid you are still a thief, Rat. What about Speckledy Hen's egg? What about the farmer's corn? Where did that jam come from, which I see on your nose? And the treacle toffee on the end of your tail?

"The knot will stay tied until you turn over a new leaf, Rat."

Owl went back to his library. He took down his book on sailing-ships, and examined the rigging.

"Quite correct in every detail," said he.

Rat hobbled painfully back through the wood, but he felt happier, for he had made something, and Owl had looked pleased with it.

The next day, as usual, he paid his visit to the farmyard. In the hen-roost was Speckledy Hen's latest egg. Rat looked at it with longing eyes. Speckledy Hen was a good-natured, silly creature. He would leave her egg. He started to go down the stair. Was it imagination? He felt a loosening in his tail.

"Cluck! Cluck!" cried the Speckledy Hen when she saw him. She ran shrieking to her precious egg. There it was, safe and sound! She couldn't understand. Had Rat turned over a new leaf?

Rat went into the barn. There was litter on the floor, and he seized a bunch of twigs and swept it away. Then he went up to the meal sack and gazed at its bulging sides.

A pity to mess up the floor again! He turned away, and another little hitch in his tail seemed to be loosened.

He went to Hedgehog's house under the hedge.

"Can I do any little thing for you, Hedgehog?" he asked.

Old Hedgehog stared. "Do you mean a little burglary?" he asked.

"No, I'll help to carry your milk pails to the neighbours," said Rat.

"And drink the milk again," replied the Hedgehog indignantly.

"Try me," said Rat, so Hedgehog trusted him with the milk for the Red Squirrel who lived up in the pine-tree.

So Rat took the milk to the Red Squirrel's door, and knocked gently. He filled the jug at the foot of the tree.

"Oh!" shouted the Red Squirrel. "A Rat! A Rat!" He fled to the top of his tree, and sat there, peeping down. When Rat was out of sight he crept down again, and looked around. His pyjamas, hanging on the clothes-line, were still there; his bowl of nuts was untouched; the milk-jug was filled.

Rat walked through the fields, keeping close to the walls. Both his heart and his tail felt lighter, and when he got back to Hedgehog's house, there was a mug of milk and a hunch of bread and cheese, waiting on the doorstep.

Fuzzypeg peeped roung the corner, all ready to run away. Rat put his hand in his pocket and brought out a dozen oak-apples, which he gave to the astonished little hedgehog for marbles.

As evening came there were sounds of gaiety in the hayfield. In the far corner Squirrel and little Grey Rabbit in blue sun-bonnets were raking the hay, and Hare was piling it up into haycocks. Hedgehog and Fuzzypeg came to help and tossed it with their prickles. Then Mole joined them, with a little hayfork.

Rat stood looking at the happy scene. He was on his way to Grey Rabbit's house, where he hoped to find the raspberry tartlets waiting for him. He wouldn't be caught this time! He knew his way about, and Squirrel was safe for an hour or two. Then he noticed the feast spread out under the hedge, not far from him. There it lay, in the shade of the foxgloves, with no one to guard it!

There was a little white cloth, and on it a basket filled with the tempting raspberry tartlets! So it was of no use to go to the house. There were nut leaves laden with wild strawberries and raspberries, and a jug full of cream. There was sloe jam, little green lettuces, and radishes like rosebuds, and a big plum cake, and the treacle toffee!

Rat's mouth watered. He stared so hard at the plum cake that he felt he could taste its delicious sugary crust. Then he turned away and walked home.

Rat gazed up at the sky, at the birds, so light and free, and at that moment he felt light and free, too. The last knot in his tail had come undone. He was a happy Rat, loosened from his fetters.

"I saw Rat staring at our feast," confided Grey Rabbit to the others. "He didn't touch a thing, and he didn't know that I saw him."

"Rat helped to carry my milk today, and he swept the barn clean too," said old Hedgehog.

"Rat gave me some marbles," cried little Fuzzypeg.

"I wonder if Wise Owl gave him some good advice," mused the Mole.

The next morning Rat came to little Grey Rabbit's house. He carried a pair of shears and a scythe and he walked with a quick light step.

"Can I mow your lawn, or cut your hedge, Grey Rabbit?" said he. "Or weed your garden?"

"Why! The knot has gone from your tail, Rat!" exclaimed Grey Rabbit.

"Who untied it, Rat?"

"No one," replied Rat, modestly.

"It came undone by itself. I'm not a thief anymore. I now understand what Wise Owl meant when he told me to turn over a new leaf. I shall work for my living, little Grey Rabbit."

He took up his shears and cut the hedge, making peacocks and balls and ships. He mowed the lawn smooth as silk, and he pulled up every tiny weed.

He went in the wood to gather sticks, and as he passed under Owl's tree, the wise bird looked out.

"Ho! Ho!" he hooted. "A reformed Rat. The knot is not! A skilful Rat! An artist! Bring me another present someday. I shall be honoured to accept it."

The Rat blushed through his dusky skin with pride, but he went on gathering his sticks.

That night he went home with his wages in his pocket, a respectable working animal.

"I'm going to carve something else," said he to his wife. "You've never seen anything like what I'm going to make!" He sat down at the table with a little white bone, and began to carve – but that is a secret for another time!